THE ADVENTURES OF BILLIE AND PILLIE

By Christopher J. Evans

Strategic Book Publishing and Rights Co.

Strategic Book Publishing and Rights Co., LLC
USA | Singapore
www.sbpra.com

For information about special discounts for bulk purchases, please contact Strategic Book Publishing and Rights Co. Special Sales, at bookorder@sbpra.net.

ISBN: 978-1-946540-91-1

Book Design: Suzanne Kelly

Weyland,
Always
Seek
Adventure!

CHAPTER 1

BUILDING THE NEST

It all happened a long, long time ago.

Mr. Pelican, tired from a two-hour trip out to sea, returned to the nest with fresh fish deep within his finely feathered throat.

Mr. Pelican had been soaring and diving in the cold Pacific Ocean waters, catching many small fish that swim in large schools just below the ocean's surface. A magnificent diver, the pelican was able to not only feed himself, but also to contain within his pouch many fish, which he would later return to the nest.

Mrs. Pelican, a beautiful brown bird, which, at eight pounds, was two pounds lighter than her husband, was sitting on a nest made from sticks, straws, grasses, and leaves. The nest was high atop a windblown shore pine, its needles facing the lee or wind-safe side from the ocean.

She had built the nest herself, although her mate had perhaps done the hard part—bringing her all of the building materials. The nest was two feet across and about ten inches deep.

The two chalky white eggs had been laid two days apart.

Mr. and Mrs. Pelican took turns sitting on the eggs, incubating them for one month. When not nest watching, the birds would fly, one at a time, far out to sea to fish for themselves or their mate. The nesting bird would spend the quiet time preening its feathers. To do that, the bird would bend its long neck back toward its tail. There, on top of the tail, is a small oil gland. By rubbing the end of its large bill on top of the gland, the bird is able to collect a few droplets of precious oil, which it then rubs throughout its fine feathers. This process is very valuable for all birds, especially for sea birds, as the oiled feathers repel water,

allowing the bird to remain dry and float on the water more easily.

With large wings, nearly seven feet from wing tip to wing tip, Mr. Pelican soared on the northwesterly winds back to the nest on the western coast of Oregon. As he approached the nest, his wife raised and wagged her long bill high toward the sky, acknowledging his presence.

Finally home, he opened his large wings and spread his tail to stop, but he still tumbled into the nest, crowding Mrs. Pelican, who was patiently sitting on the two beautiful eggs. She almost had to laugh at his approach, but realized, as with all pelicans, landings are not one of their most graceful traits acts.

Just inside the nest, Mr. Pelican brought up some small fishes from his throat. Mrs. Pelican quickly stepped off the nest, as she was very tired and hungry from her long spell at nesting. She quickly devoured the meal brought in by her mate.

Mr. Pelican gently moved into the nest and carefully covered the two eggs. As he settled in, he ruffled up his feathers so that the eggs could best receive the warmth from the hot, hidden skin of his body.

Mrs. Pelican, about to leave the nest, shrieked with wonderful pelican sounds, and then flew off to sea with great pride and conviction. She knew that the many days of incubating would soon be over.

After another two hours of time, Mrs. Pelican, with her belly full of fish, returned to the nest for the final watch of the night. The sun had just set, and the beautiful pink and purple light that it gave out reflected on the ocean's surface. The breezes had calmed and nightfall was fast approaching. The chill in the air prompted Mrs. Pelican to fluff up her feathers, so much so that her body and wings completely covered the nest. While she was incubating the eggs, Mr. Pelican roosted on a nearby tree branch, his pride showing as he occasionally raised his bill and let out a melodious call.

Both pelicans were very tired, but they knew that hatching time was soon to come.

CHAPTER 2

THE HATCHING

It was not long after the morning sun painted the sky and the sea a brilliant pink and crimson that the first egg began to crack open. Slowly, oh so slowly, the egg's firm shell was pecked by the young bird, still deep in darkness. Using the "egg-tooth," a small projection on top of the upper bill, the little pelican managed to make a small opening, allowing fresh air to enter the egg chamber and giving the little bird a bit more energy.

Almost an hour passed before the little bird broke the bounds of the shell and was able to get his first glimpse of his mother and father, and, oh, how proud they were! They named him Billie, after their favorite uncle.

Billie lay motionless in the nest for quite some time, allowing his feathers to dry and his body to become accustomed to the breezes from the sea, although his mother's warm body still sheltered him from the cold.

He would not need to eat soon, as mother nature had provided him with enough food in the remaining "egg yolk" within his body, which gave him strength for a couple of days before he would need to gain nourishment from the fish brought to him by his parents.

It was just two days later that the second egg began the same process of cracking. The little bird that emerged, whose name was to become Pillie (named after another favorite uncle), fought and struggled with great determination. It was almost as though he could sense that he was not the first to hatch and, therefore, had some catching up to do.

After a few hours of rest, Pillie made his move. Acting like a cuckoo chick would, he tried to get under his brother's belly and throw him out of the nest. It was unbelievable that a little pelican chick could be so rascally and yet, as you will see, that was to be the nature of Pillie, the second pelican chick to be hatched from the nest high above the ground.

CHAPTER 3

LITTLE FEATHERS SOON APPEAR

It took a few days before the soft, downy, pre-feather coat protecting each young chick began to fall out. Think about the puffy little seeds of the dandelion flower—the little wisps of puff that you blow into the wind. That is how the pre-feather coat of the baby pelican looked. This coat is replaced by many, many small beautiful light white feathers. It would be a couple of more months before the white feathers would be replaced by mature brown feathers, like those of the parent birds. Billie's new feather coat was the first to appear.

The two young pelicans were watched over carefully by their parents, so Pillie's bad behavior had to stop. Pillie had to learn how to get along with his two-hour-older brother, Billie. This was something it seemed that Pillie could do, except when it came time for dinner. For their first dinner of fresh ocean fish, Pillie attempted to get as many of the little fish as he could, until his brother Billie complained to his father, who had brought in the nice fishy dinner.

"Daddy," Billie said in pelican language, "Pillie is eating more than his fair share of fish. I am still hungry."

"Now, now, Billie, I am sure your younger brother will soon learn to share. Let us give him a second chance," said Mr. Pelican.

"Okay, Daddy," said Billie, "I will give him a second chance."

All seemed to being going well for the young pelicans. Each day Mr. and Mrs. Pelican not only brought their sons fish to eat, but also made sure they were kept warm from the cool ocean breezes.

It was not too long before the young pelicans' new brown feathers were long and strong. It was now time for Mr. and Mrs. Pelican to teach their young how to prepare for their first flight from the nest.

It was obvious that much practice time was needed by the young pelicans before they could leave the nest. Fortunately, since pelicans are such large birds, the young remain in the nest for up to three months. It is during the final month in the nest that they must practice and practice the motions of flight. In fact, they needed to flap their wings many, many times each day before their flight muscles were strong enough to lift them into the air.

Billie was very good at taking short practices, allowing his muscles to rest after each exercise. Pillie, on the other hand, worked so hard and so long during each pre-flight attempt that he would tire himself out and then be forced to sit at the bottom of the nest with his bill open wide, gasping for air. Boy, would he never learn?

The next day was to be a big day for one of these young pelicans. One pelican would make a mistake of a lifetime. Which pelican do you think it will be?

CHAPTER 4

THE TAKE OFF

A few days later, Mr. and Mrs. Pelican noticed that the two boys had been practicing their flight maneuvers while still in the nest. "I think it is time for the boys to fly today," Mrs. Pelican said to Mr. Pelican.

"Yes, I think so too," he replied.

So, with the boy's hearts pounding it was time to fly.

Billie, being the older of the two boys, was the first to try. He perched upon the edge of the nest, opened his beautiful brown wings, and jumped into the air. "I can fly, I can fly, I can fly!" the little pelican shouted. And so he did. Around and around the nesting tree he flew, each time a little faster and a little stronger. "Mom, Dad, I can fly!" shouted the young bird.

"Yes you can," replied his parents in unison.

Billie soon returned to the nest, tired but very proud. Now it was Pillie's turn.

Now remember, Pillie did not exercise properly and therefore was not in the best physical condition. However, he did climb to the edge of the nest and, with lots of pride, jumped up and out of the nest.

Pillie flapped and flapped his wings, but they did not support his weight, and soon down and down he went, until he found himself crashing into a sand dune a few feet away from the base of the nesting tree. "Mom! Dad!" Pillie yelled. "Please come and help me."

The two parent birds quickly flew to Pillie and tried their best to calm down the young bird. In the meantime, Billie, high up in the nesting tree, had to keep his pouch shut so as not to laugh at his younger brother.

"Mom, Dad, what should I do? How can I get up into the air and into the nest again?" asked Pillie.

Mr. Pelican had just the answer for his younger son. "Pillie, you must climb up to the top of this sand dune. Once on top, you can jump up and away from the sand, and you will be in the air again."

So with his father's advice, Pillie slowly climbed the steep sand dune, jumped up and away, and was soon back into the air and into the nest.

"Boy, I sure need to exercise more," Pillie exclaimed. "I need to be strong like Billie!" Pillie settled into the nest, closed his eyes, and soon was fast asleep.

CHAPTER 5

AN OILY MESS!

It was a warm, sunny day at the coast. Light winds were blowing, and the air temperature was a pleasant sixty-five degrees. Our pelican family took advantage of the great day to make a long flight up and down the coast, looking for schools of fresh fish along the way.

Billie and Pillie were enjoying flying with their parents. It was one of the few times that all four family members were up in the air at the same time. Mr. Pelican used this time to teach the young birds a few lessons about diving and flying.

To see an adult brown pelican flying high in the sky is remarkable. When not fishing, the large bird can fly several thousand feet high in the sky. So high, in fact, that if you did not know better, you might mistake a high-flying pelican for an airplane.

When fishing, the brown pelican must fly much closer to the ocean surface in order to spot sustenance, or fish in this case. The brown pelican is only one of seven species that plunges from as high as sixty-five feet down into the water to catch its prey. When it hits the water, it has its pouch closed and only opens it when in the water. To hit the water with its mouth open would be a physical catastrophe because their beaks would be torn apart.

As they flew along, Mr. Pelican spotted a shiny patch of ocean about two hundred yards ahead of them. As they grew closer, Mr. Pelican realized that the shiny spot was a patch of oil, which must have come from a leaking ship.

Billie and Pillie were interested in knowing more about this rare sighting (rare for them anyway). "Be very careful, boys," stated Mr. Pelican. "Never, ever dive into the water when it looks like that. For what you see floating on top of the water is called an oil patch."

"Why? Why can't we do that?" the boys asked together.

"Because, if you get oil on your feathers, you would not be able to fly, and soon you would get so tired that you would not even be able to swim, and then you would sink into the water and die," Mr. Pelican stated with emotion.

"Don't worry," answered Billie, "we would never do that."

"That's right," echoed Pillie, but his voice was soft and not too convincing.

Soon it was time to return to the nest. Mr. and Mrs. Pelican and Billie made a sharp turn to the east and headed toward home.

Pillie, however, was so fascinated with the patch of oil that he just had to get a closer look. So, when his mother and father and brother were not looking, Pillie quietly turned around and headed right back to that oily patch on the ocean's surface. Once he was directly above it, he tucked in his wings and made a super-fast dive straight down into the murky oil patch. Down and down he dove, faster and faster, farther and farther. With wings tucked in tight, Pillie hit the oil patch so hard that he went through the oil patch and into the water to a depth of about three feet. Seconds later, his body shot right back up to the oily coated surface.

Right away Pillie realized that it was almost impossible to swim in the thickened mess. With a big struggle, Pillie soon understood that with his feathers coated in the heavy, gooey oil it was impossible to fly.

There was nothing for Pillie to do but cry. And cry he did, with his salty tears making little marks on the oily surface. (Oh, and yes, in case you are wondering, pelicans *do* cry, as they have special salt glands that allow them to tolerate the ingestion of sea water.)

In the meantime, the pelican family became concerned about their missing son and brother. "Where can he be?" asked Mr. Pelican. "I'd better fly back to where we last saw him. And

I do hope that he did not do anything crazy, like diving into the oil patch!"

So, Mr. Pelican left the nest and started the half-hour flight back to the site where they last saw Pillie. Once Mr. Pelican had covered the distance from the nest to the oil patch, he could see something splashing around in the oil. Could it be Pillie?

Sure enough, it was Pillie. As Mr. Pelican flew circles around Pillie, he yelled, "Calm down and don't try to swim or fly. Your feathers are coated with oil, and you will not be able to do anything but tread water. Be patient, and I will go find the coast guard and seek their help getting you out of this mess, a mess that you got yourself into."

And so Mr. Pelican flew back to the Oregon Coast where the coast guard base was located.

Now, of course, the men from the coast guard could not understand pelican language, but they certainly could understand a pelican in distress.

Mr. Pelican flew right up to the three men in uniform. As he landed in front of them, he jumped up and down, flapping his wings over and over again.

Well, it did not take long for the three gentlemen from the coast guard to realize that something was very wrong. "I think that pelican needs our help," said one of the men.

"Yes, I think you are right," said the second man. "I think we should take the helicopter, in case this is a rescue. We need to escort this pelican to the source of trouble as soon as possible."

"Hey, wait a minute" stated the third man. "I received a call on the emergency phone just a couple of minutes ago about a ship out at sea leaking oil. I'll bet this pelican is trying to tell us something that is linked to that oil spill."

With a potential devastation in mind, a coast guard leaned over and grabbed Mr. Pelican, gently lifting him up and placing him under his sheltering arms.

With Mr. Pelican safely stowed, the coast guard ran to the helicopter, opened the doors, buckled up, started the rotation of the large helicopter blades, and headed for the oil slick. Would they make it in time?

CHAPTER 6

LIFT OFF!

The Oregon coast guard rescue helicopter was a Eurocopter HH-65 Dolphin. It had a height of thirteen feet and was thirty-eight feet long. Its four rotors had a diameter of over thirty-nine feet. The short-range recovery helicopter had a crew of three and could fly up to four hours before refueling. The helicopter was used to perform search and rescue, law enforcement, and security missions. This was a mighty big and expensive piece of aircraft to search and rescue a pelican, but it was the coast guard's mission to save lives and, well, Pillie the pelican did have one. So, as the mighty helicopter became airborne, it swung around, rose above the shore pine trees, and set its compass to a west-northwest direction.

A half-mile up and about one mile out to sea, the helicopter had traveled only ten minutes before the crew of the flight spotted the oil slick.

Now, you may think that ten minutes is a short time for the flight crew to arrive at the problem site, but remember, the speed of the aircraft, at one hundred ninety miles an hour, was much greater than the speed of our feathered pelican family.

We know that there are three coast guard members in the helicopter: the pilot, the co-pilot, and the spotter. It was the job of the spotter to actually "spot" Pillie. So, with binoculars in place, the spotter looked north and south, east and west, until finally, approximately one-hundred yards ahead, he saw a bird stuck in the oil, flapping his wings (or at least trying to) with all of his might.

"Bird ahead!" yelled the spotter. "Location, two hundred eighty degrees north-northwest," he added.

The excited pilot and copilot soon spotted the pelican too and quickly slowed the helicopter's rotary blades, which allowed the *heli*, as a helicopter is frequently called, to begin a descent to the ocean surface below.

In the meantime, Mr. Pelican, who was sitting on top of a seat directly behind the pilot, had been anxiously peering out of the second window, desperately searching for any sign of his son.

"Oh, I see him! I see him!" yelled Mr. Pelican, but, of course, the coast guard could not understand a single squawk the bird emitted.

Jumping up and down, Mr. Pelican was now so excited that he could hardly stand it. "Yes, it is Pillie! I can see him!" he shouted again. *But how are they going to get him into this noisy flying machine?* he wondered.

CHAPTER 7

PILLIE GOES HOME

As the helicopter slowly descended, the wind from the router blades caused the ocean water around Pillie to froth up like whipped cream on top of a mug of hot chocolate.

Now, with all of this commotion going on, life was not at all comfortable for Pillie, and, in fact, he was very frightened. *Oh how I wish I had never plunged into this oil patch*, thought Pillie. *I need to always respect whatever Mom and Dad tell me.*

And so, cold and wet and scared to death, Pillie could only wait in anticipation.

Looking up at the helicopter, Pillie noticed that a door on the side of the helicopter had opened and a wire *rescue basket* was being lowered over the side of the craft. Slowly, the basket approached him, swinging back and forth in the Pacific Ocean wind. Closer and closer it came, and Pillie could see a coast guard inside the caged basket. This highly trained man had taken many hours of rescue classes, which gave him the knowledge and skill necessary to rescue people who are in grave danger.

Yes, he was trained to rescue people, not pelicans.

But there he was, just inches now from reaching poor Pillie, who was scared and cold from his long ordeal.

Slowly the man in the basket came to Pillie. At first he was a few yards away, and then a few feet away, and finally just inches away. The coast guard reached out to grab the poor young bird, but suddenly a giant orca, also known as a killer whale, rose to the surface, its long dorsal fin rising four feet above the ocean's surface.

CHAPTER 8

UP FROM THE DEPTHS

Orcas are big—really, *really* big. A full-grown killer whale, which orcas are also called, can weigh more than six tons and be as much as twenty-six feet long. Because of its size and strength, it can swim up to thirty-five miles per hour. As orcas are mammals, they are very smart and often hunt in pods, sort of the way wolves hunt in packs. In a pod, the orcas are able to surround their prey, such as seals, sea lions, salmon, and even larger whales.

With that information, should we be afraid of what this orca might do to poor Pillie and the coast guard? Well, not really, as orcas don't normally feed on birds and are not considered a threat to humans.

So, why do you think this orca came to the surface so close to Pillie and the coast guard trying to rescue him? Well, it is probably because orcas are very intelligent animals. They can be very curious and like to play, just like your pet dog might like to do.

It might have seemed like an hour, but after just a few seconds, the orca, having viewed the rescue, decided that the excitement was over, and down, down into the ocean's depths it disappeared.

The coast guard reached out and grabbed Pillie, gently placing him into the wire basket. The coast guard had placed a warm blanket in the basket and quickly wrapped it around the young bird to keep him warm. The coast guard then signaled for the helicopter copilot to turn on the motor that would raise the basket back into the helicopter.

Slowly the basket was pulled up from the ocean's surface until it was close enough for the copilot to swing it into the open door of the helicopter. Pillie was saved.

With the helicopter door now closed, the heli turned to the east and headed back to the coast guard station. Pillie's father, who had been observing all of this, was now so excited and relieved that his son was alive and not too badly hurt, that he found himself shedding several tears. But these were tears of relief that this whole ordeal was almost over.

Now, the only thing that was really hurt was Pillie's pride. Once again he had done something unfortunate and had to learn a lesson.

CHAPTER 9

THE PUMPKIN PATCH

It was the month of October. In the valley and on the coast, the evergreen trees retained their needles, but the broadleaf trees saw their leaves turning beautiful colors. Orange, yellow, red, purple, and brown pigments suddenly appeared from beneath the dominant green chlorophyll package that color the leaves for most of the year.

Billie and Pillie, refreshed after a good night's sleep, awoke to see their mom and dad standing proudly beside them. They stretched their muscles and flapped their wings; it would soon be time for breakfast. Fortunately for them, Mr. Pelican had just returned from a journey along the coastal waters, and within his pouch was a bundle of fresh herring, the favorite food of pelicans.

Pillie, being the more aggressive of the two brothers, forced his chattering bill into his father's pouch to take the first big gulp of food! Poor Billie would just have to wait (as always). But soon, Billie too was able to enjoy the fishy breakfast, and boy was it ever tasty.

After breakfast, the boys soon were asking their parents what the plan was for the day. "Will we fly out to sea as usual?" asked Billie.

"No, no, no," piped in Pillie. "I want to fly into the valley."

"Yes, we could do that," responded their father. "The beautiful colors of the fall season are here—all of the leaves turn colors before they break off from the tree limbs and gently float to the waiting earth below."

"Hurray, hurray!" trumpeted Pillie. "I have always wanted to fly inland instead of out to sea. We always fly over the ocean and never have we flown into the valley."

Pillie was right, pelicans rarely fly inland. After all, the fish are in the sea, not on the land.

So, off to the east the pelican family flew, higher and higher, until they were actually above the low coastal clouds.

It was a beautiful October morning. The sun had been up for only a couple of hours, and the foggy mist was rising from the rich, moist soil of the valley floor.

Forty minutes passed, and it was time for the pelican family to begin its descent into the valley. The boys were very excited to be dropping in elevation, for now they could stretch out their wings without flapping them—not even one beat—and glide down to earth.

With keen eyes, all four of the pelicans surveyed the landscape below, searching for anything interesting they would not normally see along the coast.

And then suddenly, there it was: a big, beautiful field of bright orange pumpkins, all shining in the early morning sun. "Wow!" was the first word Billie uttered. "What a wonderful sight," he added.

"Oh, yes," were the excited words of Pillie. "Mom, Dad, let us glide down and have our breakfast."

"Oh no, Pillie. Pelicans are meant to eat fresh fish, not fresh pumpkins," replied his parents, both with beaky grins.

But Pillie paid no attention—there was trouble brewing. Without so much as a squawk, Pillie dove down toward the pumpkin patch as though he were diving after a school of herring. And then . . . *wham!* . . . he struck a large orange pumpkin with his pouched beak, driving it deep into the pumpkin's center! Down on the ground, with a pumpkin stuck over his face clear up to his eyeballs, Pillie looked and felt ridiculous.

"Help! Help me!" Pillie attempted to yell, though it was hard to hear his cry, as it sounded like it was coming from a deep cave.

But Mom, Dad, and Billie soon saw his plight and dropped down to his rescue.

Mr. Pelican, being the biggest and strongest, grabbed the stem of the pumpkin and Mother and Billie each held onto one of Pillie's webbed feet. Together they all pulled and pulled until finally . . . *pop!* . . . poor Pillie was rescued from a potential disaster once again. Would Pillie ever learn?

CHAPTER 10

POOR PILLIE'S STOMACH

Pelicans eat fish and other kinds of seafood like squid, mussels, and clams. Do you think pelicans would ever eat pumpkins? Well, certainly not, and that is just what Mr. and Mrs. Pelican told Pillie, but you know Pillie. You could talk to him until you were blue in the face, and Pillie just would not listen. No, he would not listen at all.

Freed from the big orange gourd, Pillie began to think. Now, you might say that having Pillie think was a great idea but, sorry, no. When Pillie thought, his thinking was normally not in his best interest, nor in the interest of anyone else for that matter.

What Pillie needed to do now, was to get his mom, dad, and brother to move a short distance away, so he could try eating the pumpkin secretly without anyone seeing him. How could he do that? He had to think of a way that was foolproof.

And then, finally, he had the perfect solution to his problem. He would scare off Mom, Dad, and Billie so he could be alone. He shouted, "Watch out! Get out of here! There are three boys with guns approaching! Run or fly for your lives!"

Well, that was enough to scare off the three pelicans. They ran to get air under their wings, and then up they lifted and quickly flew to the top of a nearby oak tree. While they were doing that, little Pillie was ramming his beak into the golden pumpkin and taking in huge amounts of pumpkin pulp—seeds and all. Bite after bite he took, and bite after bite he swallowed, until he could eat no more.

With a full tummy, he looked up to see his family perched in the oak tree a safe distance away. Now it was time to join them. So Pillie began his run before his usual leap into the air to fly to

Christopher J. Evans

the tree to join the pelican trio, but there was one little problem. Actually, it was a very big problem.

For you see, poor Pillie had eaten so much that his heavy, enlarged belly would not allow him to get into the air. Time after time he ran and leaped, ran and leaped, but no—leaping into the air was out of the question. He was grounded. Only after several hours of waiting for his body to process his heavy meal, would he be able to fly once again.

Soon, nighttime approached and, with it, the cooler air that settles onto the valley floor. Poor Pillie fluffed up his feathers and strained his eyes to get a last peek at his mother, father, and brother still perched in the distant oak tree. He could see that they were all huddled closely together, conserving body heat. Oh, how he wished he could be with them. If only he had paid attention to his parents. *Pelicans are meant to eat fresh fish and not fresh pumpkins.* With that harsh reminder from his parents, Pillie lay down on his distended belly, tucked his head under his wing, and, with a great struggle, was finally able to fall asleep, hoping tomorrow would be a better day.

CHAPTER 11

THE VERDICT IS IN

When the autumn sun finally climbed up over the Cascade Mountains, sending its warm rays down into the valley, young Pillie awoke with the great fear that he might still be grounded and unable to fly.

Well, there was only one way to find out, and that was to get up and run, run, and run, and then jump into the air to achieve pelican lift off.

That he did . . . well, *run* anyway. Nope, he was still too heavy to take flight. Thus, the only thing he could do was cry. Soon his cries and shouts of "Help me!" were carried by the morning breezes to the top of the oak tree where his family was still huddled.

Mr. Pelican was the first to hear Pillie's call and immediately alerted Mrs. Pelican and Billie. Together the three pelicans hurriedly jumped off their perch and drifted down to Pillie, only one hundred yards or so away.

Upon seeing his grounded son, Mr. Pelican asked Pillie what had happened. Through tears, Pillie told his father the whole truth. After all, what else could he do? Pillie then asked, "Dad, what can I do? How can I ever lose enough weight to fly again? Dad, Mom, and Billie, I am so, so sorry. What I did will never happen again. I just want to fly with the three of you and do what pelicans are supposed to do," squawked Pillie.

"Oh, Pillie, I know what you can do to lose that weight and get back into the air," said Mr. Pelican, with a glint of surprise in his eye. "What? What is it?" asked Pillie, with desperation in his voice.

"It's called exercise, my son, exercise. Only by working out really hard over the next couple of days will you be able to lose those pumpkin pounds that you have put on your body. Only by exercising and eating the proper foods, which of course would be fish, can you hope to get yourself back into the air."

"Okay, Daddy. I promise I will work really hard, and I am so sorry about all the bad things that I have done. That will never happen again, I promise," whimpered Pillie, in a voice that was hard to hear.

Well, do you think Pillie will keep his word and exercise hard enough to fly again? And do you think Pillie will keep his promise to be a good pelican once and for all?

CHAPTER 12

PELICANS DON'T DO PUSHUPS!

Normally when children go to the gym or the playground to do their exercises, they might just start with jumping jacks. Well, pelicans are normally very good at doing jumping jacks, and young Billie was exceptionally good. In fact, when he jumped up, he lifted his wings up high and his legs would spread apart. And then, when he pushed his wings down, his legs and feet came together, he would actually lift up a couple of feet off the ground. Yes, the powerful down stroke of his wings would send air down and his body up. It was really fun doing jumping jacks, and it was beautiful to see. But, pushups? Well, that is a different matter. For you see, pelicans don't do pushups.

Why don't they do pushups? The answer to that is easy: pelicans don't have hands! It is very difficult to do a pushup when you do not have hands.

So Billie did several jumping jacks and followed that with a few wind sprints. Now it was Pillie's turn to exercise. Which exercise would he try to do?

You guessed it. Pillie was going to try to do a pushup. Oh, brother.

Pillie was determined, very determined, to prove to his mother, father, and especially his brother, that he really could do a pushup. It was all a matter of putting into practice what Pillie was imagining in his head. Why couldn't he do a pushup? After all, children do them all the time.

The problem, of course, was that Pillie was not a child, but rather a bird. Yes, a bird, and birds are not constructed to do pushups. It is just that they do not have hands, and without hands, how can you support your upper body and lift it up off the ground?

Well, if you know your anatomy, and of course Pillie did not know his anatomy, then you will know that the bones of a bird's wing and the bones of a person's arm are really quite similar. That is, the bones in the wing are the same as the bones in a person's arm.

A person has one bone in the upper arm and two bones in the lower arm. And guess what? The bones in the wing of a bird are just the same. It is only the bones of a person's hand and the bones in the tip of the bird's wing that are a bit different, but that shouldn't matter should it? Well, not for Pillie anyway.

When his family was not looking, Pillie lay on the ground and positioned his body so that the second portion of his wing (like the forearm in people) lay flat under his chest.

With great concentration, Pillie slowly and carefully pushed his lower wing down on the earth's soil, and, as he did so, his body slowly, very slowly, lifted upward. Yes, oh yes, Pillie had done it! Pillie had done a pushup, probably the first pushup in all of bird history. Good job, Pillie.

CHAPTER 13

A COLD NORTHWESTERLY RAIN STORM APPROACHES

You learned earlier that birds that spend a lot of time on or around water have a very special adaptation. They all have an important gland on the top of their tails which, when rubbed, secretes several drops of thick oil. This oil, when picked up by the bird's bill, is transferred to the bird's feathers and keeps water from soaking into the bird's feathered coat. Isn't Mother Nature wonderful?

It was soon after young Billie and Pillie grew their first coat of fine feathers that Mr. Pelican told the boys all about the oil gland—what it is for and how it is designed. He stressed to them how important it was to take a few drops of oil from the gland each day and rub the oil throughout their feathers. If this special oil, not to be confused with an oil slick in the ocean, was not applied to their feathers, then the feathers would not be able to repel water properly, and the bird's body would get wet and cold.

As you can probably imagine, Billie took his father's advice very seriously and worked on spreading oil from his oil gland to his feathers every time he had a spare minute. At first he found that this oil-spreading was not so easy to do, but with lots of practice, Billy soon mastered the art of oil-spreading, and soon all of his feathers were water-repellent.

But then there was Pillie. Although Pillie had heard what his father told him about the oil gland and all, he did not consider it important. Soon, after only a couple of days actually, what his father had told him was forgotten.

Boy, now that was a big, big mistake, for a very cold, wet, northwesterly rainstorm was heading toward the pelican family.

Mr. and Mrs. Pelican and little Billie were all prepared for the storm. Those three birds had carefully spread the precious oil from their oil glands onto their coat of feathers. But had brother Pillie done the same? Of course he had not. And because he had not done so, little Pillie was about to suffer through a long and very cold night.

CHAPTER 14

THE NORTHWESTERLY SOAKS PILLIE'S FEATHERS

Dusk had come and gone, and the last bit of sunlight had disappeared below the horizon. The pelican family prepared for the long night ahead by ruffling up their feathers, which would trap air and help keep them warm and dry throughout the dark, cold, and very wet hours ahead—*oops!*—that is, if each pelican's coat of feathers had been properly coated with that special oil we have been talking about.

Now we know that Mr. and Mrs. Pelican and little Billie had done the right thing by coating their feathers with oil—*preening*, as it is called. But then we have little Pillie, who had not done what he had been told to do by his father.

And then came the storm, which carried with it extremely strong winds and lots and lots of heavy, cold rain.

As the rain fell and struck the backs of the pelicans, it simply slipped off everyone's feathers, except Pillie's, of course. As his feathers had not been carefully preened, each drop of water that landed on Pillie went directly through his feathers and landed right on his warm skin.

Well, soon his skin was no longer warm, but rather very cold. Poor Pillie presently began to shiver, and there was nothing he could do to get himself warm. He would just have to wait until morning and hope that the warmth of the rising sun would ease his suffering.

In the meantime, Pillie cried and cried, and shortly was apologizing to his father for not paying proper attention.

Once again, Pillie had learned a very important lesson: listen to your parents, for they are very wise.

CHAPTER 15

SPRING FINALLY ARRIVES

As the morning sun slowly warmed the air, little Pillie managed to fluff up his feathers and get his body temperature back to normal. He had learned a tough lesson once again and was now determined to make this new day a day of firsts.

First, he told himself that he would always follow the directions given to him by his mom and dad.

Second, he told himself that he would respect and learn from his older brother, Billie.

And third, he told himself that, since this was such a nice and warm spring morning, he, Mr. Pillie Pelican, would make this day the first day of a new and perfect life.

Well, that is what he told himself anyway, but, unfortunately, his wishes and determination soon fell apart.

It all began as he looked up at the sky and saw a beautiful seagull soaring high above the ocean waves. Oh, how magnificent that seagull looked, just soaring and soaring away. The seagull's flight seemed effortless, for not once in a span of two or three minutes did Pillie see that seagull flap its wings. In fact, the seagull appeared to be supported by an invisible cable or something that allowed it to fly around and around, appearing not to use any effort to stay way up in the sky. Oh, how graceful that seagull looked. Could Pillie do that too?

Of course he could, or so Pillie thought.

Now, all birds have wings and feathers and two feet, of course, but not all birds can fly—penguins can't fly, for example—but the way that flying birds do fly can be very different from one bird to another.

A hummingbird, for example, can stay in one place while in flight and can even fly backward. Some birds are very fast, like swallows and falcons. And then some birds are really good at soaring or flying for long periods of time without once flapping their wings. Examples of soaring birds include buzzards, vultures, albatrosses, seagulls, and, yes, even pelicans.

Birds that are great at soaring tend to have very long wings and a lightweight body for their size. Now, Pillie did have long wings, but his body . . . well, let's just say that he had been eating too many second helpings of fish each day, and his weight was a bit on the heavy side. (His brother's weight was just right, of course). So, soaring high in the air for long periods of time might be a bit difficult for young Pillie, but we know that once Pillie makes up his mind to do something, it is almost impossible for anyone to tell him otherwise.

As Pillie continued to watch that seagull soaring way up in the sky, he no longer just wished he could soar. It was time for him to jump off of his nest, and, with all of his effort, fly high into the sky and start soaring away.

Wow, with all of his energy spent just thinking about what he planned to do, Pillie now felt very sleepy and decided to take a little morning nap. After his morning nap, he would take to the air and soar, just like that wonderful seagull. Would Pillie be able to do it? We shall soon see.

CHAPTER 16

PILLIE PREPARES TO SOAR

Pillie's little nap lasted much longer than the young pelican had planned. The sun was now on the western side of the tree tops, and its bright rays cast long shadows on the eastern side of the trees and the nest. It was no longer morning, but rather late in the afternoon.

Shaking his head to clear the cobwebs, Pillie quickly remembered that he had a quest awaiting him: he was to soar high in the sky like the seagull he had seen earlier in the morning. Soaring would be easy, Pillie thought. After all, he was a bird, he had long, strong wings, and, most important of all, he had the determination to do whatever he wanted.

Yes, that is what Pillie thought. But there was a major problem of which Pillie was totally unaware. Remember, it is now afternoon, and in the afternoon on the Oregon Coast, the winds can do some unexpected things.

As the air above the ocean heats up, coastal winds can develop. These winds can often become very strong, creating large waves with rolling tops, which become thin as they roll. These thin waves can turn into a beautiful, light-green color as they peak and crash with foamy spray. Often these crashing waves make a thunderous sound. You might think that the sound would serve as a warning to beware of the possible dangers that the ocean can bring.

These winds also push inward to the shores, and the clouds they carry often contain huge amounts of moisture, which will drop large amounts of rain upon reaching land.

Did Pillie know any of this? No, he did not, and, even if he did, do you think he would care? Probably not.

It was time for Pillie to take to the skies and soar like that seagull he had seen earlier in the morning. But, it was no longer morning, and the warm rising air currents, as well as the winds that would result because of those currents, would create a real problem for Pillie.

Never mind, it was time for Pillie to take off, to soar . . . or so he thought.

CHAPTER 17

PILLIE RIDES THE WINDS

"Oh, yeah, that seagull thinks he is hot stuff," Pillie mumbled to himself. *Well, I can fly higher and faster than that old bird*, Pillie thought.

So, with glorious visions in his mind, Pillie jumped as high as he could from the nest and soon was flapping his wings wildly. Up and up Pillie flew until he soon found that he was actually up into the clouds, the very clouds that he had just viewed from the solid foundation of his nest.

As he emerged from the cloud layer, he could sense that he was moving forward from high above the sea to the solid shores of the coast at a very alarming rate. Yes, the mighty winds were carrying little Pillie at a speed much faster than he had ever flown before. So fast, in fact, that the normally smooth feathers along his back were now pointing forward toward his shoulders.

Oh my, thought Pillie, *I think I am going a little too fast.* Boy, was that ever an understatement.

Yes, the strong ocean winds were now forcing Pillie to fly so fast that he was no longer in control of his flight. The winds were tossing him through the skies like a tumbleweed bouncing across the dry lands of Texas.

"Mommy! Daddy!" cried Pillie. "Please help me! I am being carried away to never-never land!"

But soon he was not in his own little jet stream. For, once the strong westerly winds reached the coastal mountains, the winds lost their strength. As a result, Pillie began to drop from the sky like a very large hail stone.

Down, down, down Pillie tumbled. Poor Pillie had been so battered by the strong winds that his wing muscles had little

energy left, and he was no longer able to fly as he normally would. Now, like a plane that has a mechanical malfunction, Pillie dropped from the sky.

Kabang! came the sound as Pillie hit the branches of a large cedar tree. *Kabang!* again when his poor, sore body bounced as it hit the ground. Now, fortunately, he really did have a lucky landing, as the ground he hit was covered with a thick layer of soft moss and young, tender, fern fronds. Thus, after only a few minutes, Pillie was able to pick himself up and, with great effort, take to the air again. But this time it was a slow and low flight back to the nest where Mother, Father, and Brother Billie were anxiously awaiting his return.

And do you think Pillie told his parents and brother the truth about what just happened? You're right—he did not, because . . . well, because he was Pillie.

CHAPTER 18

BILLIE AND PILLIE CELEBRATE THEIR BIRTHDAY

It was hard to believe that Billie and Pillie would soon be celebrating their very first birthday. As the day advanced, the brother pelicans approached their mother and father and asked if they might be able to invite a couple of their best pelican friends over for their first birthday party.

"Mom! Dad!" shouted the brothers. "May we please have a birthday party? Please, please," they begged.

"Well," said Mr. Pelican, "both you boys have been very good this past year, so I guess a birthday party might be in order."

Deep in Mr. Pelican's thoughts, he knew what he had just said was not altogether true—the part about both of the boys being good. You know what he was really thinking: While Billie had indeed been a very good pelican, his brother, Pillie, had not been the perfect angel. But Mr. Pelican thought that if he threw a party just for Billie, then Pillie would really be upset and most likely get himself into even more trouble.

Therefore, Mr. Pelican talked to Mrs. Pelican, and they told the boys that, yes, they could have a party for their first birthday, and each could invite one of their closest friends.

"Yes! Yes!" screamed the boys. "We are going to have a big party for our first birthday. Thank you, Dad! Thank you, Mom! You won't be sorry for your decision. We will be very good hosts and share everything with our friends. We promise."

Now, please remember that they said they would share everything with their birthday friends. Certainly there should not be any problem with this arrangement . . . or will a certain someone make a real mess out of everything? What do you think might happen?

CHAPTER 19

HOW MANY FISH TO CATCH?

M rs. and Mr. Pelican sat down with the boys a few days before the party to discuss what special activities the boys thought would be fun to do with their invited guests.

"I think we should see who can fly the highest," suggested Pillie.

"Good idea," Mr. Pelican agreed.

"And I think we should have a contest to see who can hold the most fish in their pouch," Billie offered.

"Excellent ideas," said Mrs. Pelican.

"And what about your birthday party food?" asked Mr. Pelican. "I could make a fishing trip and catch some delicious party food if you like."

The boys thought that was a great idea. Subsequently, Mr. Pelican talked to Mrs. Pelican, and the parents agreed that, since there would be a total of four young pelicans at the birthday party, twelve fish would be the proper number for Mr. Pelican to catch. That way, each of the young birds would have three fresh fish to eat. Mr. and Mrs. Pelican wanted to make sure the young pelicans had a great party, which meant that everyone would have just the right amount of food to eat, but not too much, as no one wanted to have any sick pelicans complaining about an upset stomach.

Once Mr. and Mrs. Pelican decided on the number of fish for each of the pelicans at the party, they called the boys together and told them of their plan.

"Billie and Pillie, your mother and I have decided that I will catch a total of twelve fish for your party, which means that you and your friends can each have three fish to eat. Not too many, just the right amount for your tummies," explained Mr. Pelican.

"That sounds like the right amount to me," said Billie.

"And how about you, Pillie? Does that seem about the right amount to you too?" Mr. Pelican asked.

"Oh sure, Dad, whatever you say," Pillie replied.

It was the *way* Pillie answered that made Mr. Pelican ruffle up his feathers a bit. There was something about the tone of Pillie's voice that concerned him. *Oh, I am sure everything will be just fine*, thought Mr. Pelican. *I should be able to trust both of my boys on such a special day. I do hope I can.*

CHAPTER 20

HOW PELICANS CATCH FISH

It was very early the next morning when Mr. Pelican flew out to sea to catch some special fish for the birthday boys and their invited guests. Mr. Pelican knew that the boys' favorite fish was herring, an oceanic fish that could often be found swimming in schools of hundreds or even many thousands. Each school of fish would usually consist of fish of a similar size, from small fish of just a couple of inches, to fish over fifteen inches in length.

Mr. Pelican knew that his two sons and their birthday friends were all hungry, growing birds, so he decided to hunt around for a school of large herring. Since the pelican pouch can hold up to three gallons of water, Mr. Pelican figured he could easily carry several large herring from the fishing spot back to shore. Of course, once he had the fish within his pouch, most of the water that came with the fish would be released.

When pelicans dive for fish, they do so by folding their wings close to their bodies and tucking their chins in so that their head and body will slice cleanly into the water. Once in the water, the bird's enormous bill opens up, allowing the bird to scoop the fish into its large, expandable pouch on the lower surface of its bill.

After flying above the cold Pacific Ocean for just a few minutes, the large, beautiful pelican spotted the school of fish that would provide him with the birthday meal he was seeking. Mr. Pelican, who dove for fish every day, was quite excited for this particular dive, knowing the fish he was about to catch would make his sons very proud of him.

Spotting the tight group of herring, Mr. Pelican did the chin-tuck and wing-fold and rapidly, like a rocket, slipped into the cold ocean water, immediately scooping up all the herring he could, including a large amount of water.

As soon as Mr. Pelican came back up to the water's surface, out came the water. What was left in his pouch was a kicking and twisting mass of fresh ocean fish. Mission completed.

Now, to quickly fly back to shore before the party started, so he could show his sons the fine catch he had just made. As he flew back, Mr. Pelican wondered exactly how many fish he had in his pouch, but judging from the weight of the catch, he knew that he had plenty of fish for all of the young birds.

CHAPTER 21

WHERE DID THE FISH GO?

Arriving back at the nest, Mr. Pelican was greeted by his son, Pillie.

"Where are Billie and your mom?" Mr. Pelican asked.

"Oh, they are over there setting up an area for some games," replied Pillie, pointing with a wing to a spot not far from the nest.

Hearing that, Mr. Pelican opened his large beak, and the herring slipped from his pouch into the nest. "Here you go, Pillie. There should be enough fish here for all of you. I am going to see if your mother and brother need my help. Why don't you count the fish and let me know how many there are, and then we can decide how many fish each of you will get for your birthday meal," he explained.

With a jump and a large wing flap, Mr. Pelican was off the nest and flying away. Now Pillie could get a closer look at his father's prize catch and do a little fish count all by himself.

"Let's see—one, two, three, four, five, six, seven, eight, nine, ten, eleven, and twelve. Yes, twelve large, beautiful herring for all of us to eat."

Pillie's eyes grew enormously large, and his feathers even twitched a bit as he thought of how delicious those fish were going to taste. Oh, how he longed to have a fish right then. Just one, you know? Just one. Yes, just one.

Pillie figured that, since no one knew how many fish his father had caught, no one would know if a fish had suddenly disappeared. Just one, Pillie figured, and with that, he quickly scooped up a herring and down his throat it went.

"Wow, that was so tasty I think I might have another, but of course just one more," Pillie reasoned.

The second fish slid down Pillie's throat even easier than the first, as did the third and fourth fish. Yes, Pillie had now eaten a total of four large herring, which meant that only eight fish remained.

Pillie knew that no one, except perhaps his father, would have any idea of what Pillie had just done, because his father had left the nest before a fish count had been taken. Only Pillie knew the original number of fish. He closed his eyes and hoped his little secret would never be discovered, and that only he, Pillie, would know what had just taken place.

"Let the party begin!" shouted Pillie.

CHAPTER 22

EIGHT DIVIDED BY FOUR

Soon after Pillie had eaten four of the twelve fish, Mr. Pelican flew back to the nest. He wanted to talk to Pillie about the games that he, Mrs. Pelican, and Billie had set up for the party. Upon reaching the nest, he saw Pillie standing over the remaining fish, never knowing, of course, the original number of fish he had brought back to the nest.

"How many fish do we have here?" asked Mr. Pelican.

"Oh, I guess there are eight fish, Dad. Say, you sure did a good job catching these fish. I am so proud of you, Dad. Yes, I am so proud of you." On and on he went. Pillie was trying to cover up the fact that he had just eaten one third of the catch, leaving only eight fish for four hungry pelicans. Well, not really *four* hungry pelicans, as Pillie certainly was not very hungry now.

Soon it was time for all of the young pelicans to eat. Mr. Pelican picked up the eight fish with his beak, tossed them into his pouch, and flew off the nest to a nice picnic spot on the ground that Mrs. Pelican had selected.

Pillie followed him down to the picnic spot. While flying down, Pillie certainly could sense the added weight to his body after eating those four big fish.

With all four birds now at the picnic site, Mr. Pelican spat the fish from his pouch to the ground and excitedly told all of the pelicans that they could begin eating.

Billie and the two invited guests eagerly picked up their first fish, tossed it into the air, and quickly swallowed the tasty herring. While the young pelicans were getting ready to grab their second fish, Mr. and Mrs. Pelican noticed that Pillie had not yet picked up his first fish.

"What is wrong, Pillie?" Mrs. Pelican asked. "You haven't eaten your first fish yet."

"Oh, haven't I?" replied Pillie. "I guess I was just daydreaming. Sorry about that, Mom," and with that response, Pillie tossed his first fish (not really, right?) into the air, and down his throat it went.

"Well, that is much better," pronounced Mr. Pelican. "Now, finish with your second fish, as your brother and friends have already eaten theirs."

"Dad, I think my tummy hurts a little bit. Do I have to eat another fish?" pleaded Pillie.

"Why, Pillie, you have eaten only one fish, and one fish is not enough for your growing body. You need to eat another just to keep up your strength," answered Mr. Pelican. "Remember, I made a special flight out to the ocean to catch all these beautiful herring for your birthday party. And besides that, you will need all the energy you can get in order to have the strength to do well in the special games we are about to play."

With that explanation from his father, Pillie somehow forced his second herring (with five already in his tummy) down his throat.

"What is the first game, Father?" Pillie asked, with a slight tone of fear in his voice. Pillie was now so full of fish that he even had a hard time talking.

"Oh, the first game is probably your favorite," rebounded his father. "It is the game that you suggested."

"And what game is that, Father?" Pillie asked in a voice that could barely be heard.

"How High Can You Fly," Mr. Pelican answered. "Let's all get ready!"

Poor Pillie. When he heard what his father said, he lowered his head and closed his eyes, as he felt the rumblings in his tummy, which was so full of fish—yes, six large herring!—that the thought of flying at all, let alone flying as high as he could, really scared him. Oh, how he wished he had not eaten all of those fish. If only he could go back in time.

What do you think Pillie would have done differently if he had known that eating all of those fish might be a major problem in his goal of winning the high-flying game?

CHAPTER 23

HOW HIGH CAN YOU FLY?

The rules for the game were quite simple: each pelican would have exactly one minute to gain as much altitude as possible. He could fly in a big circle or fly in a tight, small circle. It didn't matter. The goal was to gain as much height as you could by the end of the minute.

Billie's and Pillie's friends, being guests to the party, were the first to try their luck at the game.

The first young pelican puffed up his feathers, did a few practice flaps, and then jumped into the air, working his wings as hard as he could to gain elevation. By the end of the time period, he had gained an altitude that was probably equal to the height of three tall trees.

"Hurray! Hurray!" yelled Billie and the other invited guest, as the first pelican glided back to the landing zone next to the picnic spot. For some reason, Pillie wasn't saying too much.

It was now time for the second invited pelican to try his luck, and he too flew about three tree-lengths up into the sky. Once he was back at the landing area, Billie asked Pillie if he wanted to go next.

"No, Billie, you go ahead. I am not quite ready to fly right now," said Pillie.

"Okay then, I am off!" replied Billie, jumping up into the air and using his strong chest muscles to flap his wings as hard as he could.

Up and up Billie climbed, until he was easily above the height of the previous two birds.

With a big pelican grin on his face, Billie came in for a landing, shouting out as he did so, "Hey, Pillie, I bet you can't beat that height! I have been working out each day for this contest, and as you all can see, the exercises that I have been doing really paid off."

"Yes, they certainly did," Mrs. and Mr. Pelican said with admiration. "Now, let's see if your brother can break your fine record."

While all of this activity was going on, Pillie had not said much, which, as you know, was not typical of him. Rather, Pillie had been sitting on the edge of the landing zone just watching his friends and brother fly.

Now the time had come, and the other three pelicans, plus Mr. and Mrs. Pelican, were all anxious to see just what Pillie could do. Would he be able to top the flight of his brother?

Yes, it was now Pillie's time to fly.

CHAPTER 24

UP, UP, AND DOWN!

As you know, Pillie liked to be the best at whatever was going on. He claimed to be able to jump farther, run faster, and fly higher than all of his pelican friends. Well, now was the time to prove what he could do.

Pillie walked over to the starting point near the picnic spot. He then began a series of warm-up exercises that took much longer than those performed by the other three pelicans combined.

He tried three pelican pushups (remember, pelicans can't do pushups), performed a few jumping jacks, and then did a series of wing flaps. It soon became apparent that all of this warm-up stuff was just Pillie's way of putting on a show in front of his brother, friends, and Mom and Dad. But, as they all knew Pillie well, they let him carry on and were polite enough not to say anything.

But after a little while, Mr. Pelican finally said, "Pillie, it is your turn to fly now. Let's not waste any more time, Son. Time to show us all just what you can do."

"Okay, Dad, here I go. Watch me now! Watch how high I can go! So high, much higher than Billie went," yelled Pillie as he jumped up and pumped his wings.

Oh no, there seemed to be a problem. Even though Pillie was flapping his wings as hard as he could, his body was not gaining much in the way of altitude. As the seconds clicked by and the one-minute time-limit fast approached, Pillie simply was not getting very high in the air. It was if his body was too heavy.

Now what could be the problem anyway? Yes, just what could be the problem?

CHAPTER 25

PILLIE LEARNS A LESSON

As the seconds ticked by, Pillie realized that there was no way he was going to fly as high as his brother had flown. He was not going to be able to fly as high as his birthday friends had flown either. In fact, Pillie was not even able to fly as high as one tree top. The reason was because of all of the fish he had eaten.

Yes, remember that while his brother and friends had each eaten two fish, Pillie had forced a total of six fish into his tummy. With the extra weight in his body, he was not able to gain the altitude the other pelicans had gained. In addition to the extra weight that Pillie was carrying, most of the oxygen-rich blood that should have been delivered to his flight muscles had instead gone to his stomach, where a very big job of food digestion was taking place.

People often talk about not swimming on a full stomach for the same reason. The body cannot do two things at once. It cannot digest a big meal and also prepare the muscles for activity at the same time.

When Pillie's time limit was up, everyone implored him to stop flying and come down to the landing area. Pillie sadly did as he was told. Upon reaching the ground, he hung his head low and tried to avoid eye-contact with everyone around him.

"Pillie, my son, what on earth happened to you? Why couldn't you fly as high as the others? In fact, you could hardly fly at all. Why?" Mr. Pelican wanted to know.

There was only one thing Pillie could do—tell the truth and reveal what had happened. He told everyone that, while he was in the nest, he had eaten four of the twelve fish Mr. Pelican had

caught and carried back to shore. He then ate two more fish when the other pelicans ate two fish. Thus, he had eaten a total of six extremely large, heavy herring.

While telling everyone the truth behind his poor flight performance, his large belly expanded even more as his digestive juices released lots and lots of gas, which filled him up like the birthday balloons hanging from nearby trees.

"I am so very sorry, everyone," Pillie softly explained as his eyes filled with tears. "Please forgive me. Please, please."

"Yes, I forgive you, Pillie," replied Mr. Pelican.

"Yes, we forgive you too," replied the rest of the pelicans in unison.

And so it ended—the contest, the birthday party, and an early chapter in the life of young Pillie and his brother, Billie.

As Billie and Pillie said goodbye to their friends, Mr. and Mrs. Pelican called the boys back to the nest. (Pillie had to work hard to make the short flight.) Once at the nest, Mr. and Mrs. Pelican talked about having another birthday party the next year and asked the boys if they had any suggestions about what they might do differently, if given the chance.

Billie suggested inviting more friends over so that they could have an even bigger party.

And what about Pillie? What did he have to say? Pillie promised not to overeat before the games began.

Would Pillie be able to keep his promise? We will just have to wait and see.

Review Requested:
If you loved this book, would you please provide a review at Amazon.com?

CPSIA information can be obtained
at www.ICGtesting.com
Printed in the USA
FFHW021119050319
50865687-56275FF